At the seashore,
where there is only sand and water and sky,
sometimes you can see things in the clouds . . .

THE
SKY
DOG
BRINTON
TURKLE

THE VIKING PRESS   NEW YORK

Viking Seafarer edition issued in 1971 by The Viking Press, Inc.,
625 Madison Avenue, New York, N.Y. 10022. Distributed in Canada
by The Macmillan Company of Canada Limited. Printed in U.S.A.

Library of Congress catalog card number: 79–85866

Pic Bk   1. Dog stories
              2. Fantasy

SBN 670–05056–3

1   2   3   4   5   75   74   73   72   71

FOR IAN

The first time the boy saw the sky dog,
it was smelling a big flower.

When he saw it again, it was chasing
a giant rabbit.

Another time, it was upside down,
and wearing a funny hat.

"I wish he belonged to me," said the boy.

"You wish who belonged to you?" said his mother.

"The dog. Don't you see him?" The boy pointed. "He's a shaggy white dog and he's riding on a duck and they're going to bump into a whale."

His mother looked and looked. Then she laughed and gave the boy a little hug. "I don't see it, dear," she said.

Summer was almost over at the beach. People were closing their cottages and moving away.

The boy burst into the kitchen where his mother was fixing breakfast.

"He came to me!" he said. "See, Mother?"

In his arms he was holding a shaggy white dog.

"Where did he come from?" his mother asked.
"From the sky!"
"Where did you find him?"
"He's mine," said the boy. "He was all
alone on the beach and he came to me
and his name is . . ."
"No, dear! He belongs to somebody else.
He already has a name. He's lost. We must
find out who he belongs to and give
him back."

The boy cried.

None of the people up and down the
beach had seen the dog before.

"Have you asked the policeman?" they
said. "Maybe he knows who the dog
belongs to."

The policeman had not seen the dog
before.

"Why don't you ask the man at the store?"
he said. "Maybe he knows who has lost a
dog."

The man at the store had not seen the dog before.

The boy's mother said to him, "If someone tells you they have lost a white dog, will you please say that the dog is at my cottage? My little boy is taking good care of him."

The man at the store said he would put a sign about the lost dog in his window.

The last days at the seashore, the boy
and the dog played games together on the
lonely beach.

The dog liked to dig in the sand with
the boy.

And splash in the water with the boy.

Most of all, he liked just being with
the boy.

When it was time to go back to the city, the boy helped his mother put their things away in suitcases and boxes.

A car drove up to the cottage.

The boy and his mother went to the door.

A man in a straw hat was standing there.

"I have lost my dog," he said. "I hear you have found a white dog."

"Yes," said the boy's mother. "My son found him on the beach."

"But he's not your dog," the boy told the man. "You'll see."

The man looked at the dog.

"You are right," he said. "That's not my dog. My dog is much bigger and has a brown ear."

On moving day, the boy's mother said to the policeman, "We are leaving. No one has taken the dog. What shall we do with him?"

"Do you want to keep him?" asked the policeman.

"Yes," said the boy. "He's mine."

"All right," said his mother. "We'll keep him. He's a nice dog. I wonder where he came from."

The boy hugged his mother and the dog all at once.

"His name is Cloudy," said the boy.

"Come, Cloudy!"

And Cloudy went along with the boy and
was his dog because they belonged together.